My Friend, the Starfinder

My Friend,

by
George Ella Lyon

the Starfinder

pictures by
Stephen Gammell

A Richard Jackson Book ★ Atheneum Books for Young Readers
New York   London   Toronto   Sydney

Atheneum Books for Young Readers
An imprint of Simon & Schuster Children's Publishing Division
1230 Avenue of the Americas, New York, New York 10020
Book design by Krista Vossen
The text for this book is set in Aikiko.
The illustrations for this book are rendered in pastel, watercolor,
colored pencil, and gouache.
Manufactured in China
First Edition
1 2 3 4 5 6 7 8 9 10
Library of Congress Cataloging-in-Publication Data
Lyon, George Ella, 1949–
My friend, the starfinder / George Ella Lyon ; illustrated by
Stephen Gammell.—1st ed.
p. cm.
"A Richard Jackson Book."
Summary: A child relates some of the wondrous tales told by an old
man who once found a falling star and stood at the end of a rainbow.
ISBN-13: 978-1-4169-2738-9
ISBN-10: 1-4169-2738-7
[1. Storytellers—Fiction. 2. Meteors—Fiction. 3. Stars—Fiction.
4. Rainbows—Fiction.] I. Gammell, Stephen, ill. II. Title.
PZ7.L9954My 2008
[E]—dc22
2006032026

For Dick and Stephen,
and
in memory of Glen Dean, the Starfinder
—George Ella

To the memory of my dear friend Meredith Charpentier
—Stephen

nce there was an old man.

I knew him

when I was no bigger than you are.

He wore old soft clothes
and sat in an old chair
on an old green porch
and told stories.

The stranger they were
the truer he looked
and I believed every one.

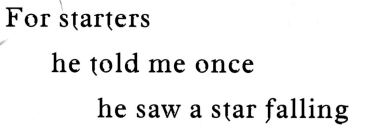

For starters

     he told me once

          he saw a star falling

and since he'd done his chores
and it was still light

he followed that star across the field.

Way, way ahead of him
it landed
so he kept walking

and when he got to the spot
he picked the star up.

It was warm and smooth
as an egg straight from the hen.

He kept it, of course. . . .

Put it in my hands—
glassy, blackish green
like puddles around a coal pile.

I held it tight
trying to feel its journey.

Another time he told me

how once he was walking along

not going anywhere in particular

when all of a sudden

he saw his hand

purple as a church window

and his arm was green—
green as this porch, he'd say—

and his old khaki pants
were red and yellow and orange as sunset
yellow and red
and orangey orange as fire.

He was at the end
of the rainbow
color pouring
over him

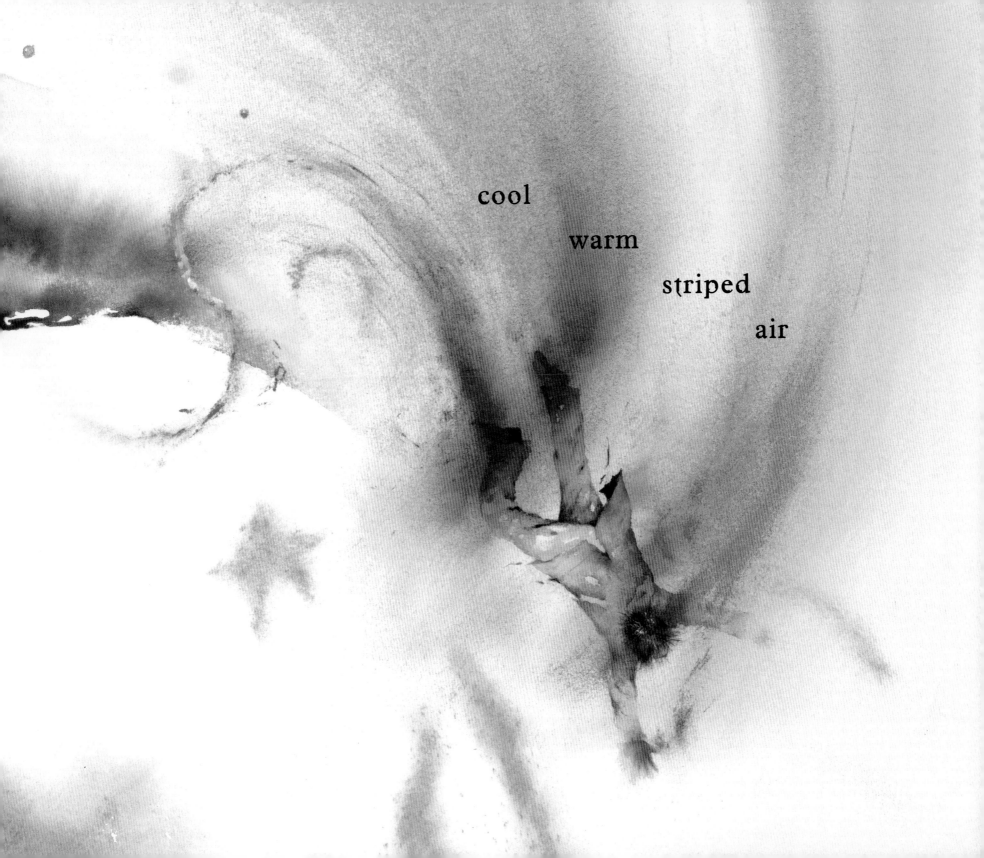

on face and hair
shirt and shoes
and belt buckle.

Now he couldn't bring home
the rainbow
the way he did the star.

But when he told the story
holding out his hand
I could feel the colors.

I could see it was true.

And how he would have to tell it
just like I'm telling you.

I knew Glen Dean, the starfinder,

from the time I was a little girl, though he didn't move to the house across the street—a house my grandfather built—until I was grown. Tall, thin, kind, and bespectacled, he worked as a heating and air-conditioning man, which is fairly cosmic when you think about it. In his retirement years he made silky-smooth furniture, including a four-poster bed for him and his wife and perfect miniature bedroom suites for his granddaughters' dolls.

Besides finding the star and winding up at the end of the rainbow, Mr. Dean had another extraordinary claim: He and his father and grandfather had lived under all the presidents of the United States. His granddaddy could have told him stories about George Washington. I know that sounds incredible, but then how many people catch a falling star?

—G. E. L.